To Mark, James, Joseph and Jessica
~ JH

To Ji-chan & Moley, with love
~ MM

SIMON AND SCHUSTER

First published in Great Britain in 2006 by Simon and Schuster UK Ltd
Africa House, 64-78 Kingsway, London WC2B 6AH

Text copyright © 2006 Julia Hubery
Illustrations copyright © 2006 Mei Matsuoka

The right of Julia Hubery and Mei Matsuoka to be identified as the author and
illustrator of this work has been asserted by them in accordance with the
Copyright, Designs and Patents Act, 1988

Book designed by Genevieve Webster
The text for this book is set in Letterpress Text
The illustrations for this book are rendered in mixed media

A CIP catalogue record for this book is available from the British Library upon request

ISBN 1 416 90399 2
EAN 9781416903994

Printed in China

1 3 5 7 9 8 6 4 2

Raffi's Surprise

Julia Hubery
& Mei Matsuoka

SIMON AND SCHUSTER
London New York Sydney

Raffi Raccoon loves his home.
He loves the long swishy grass, the sparkling
stream and the rustling, rippling trees.
But best of all, Raffi loves . . .

. . . Old Father Oak!

Raffi was born in a cosy den,
high in Father Oak's sturdy trunk.
He learned to climb on Father Oak's
strong branches in the spring.

And all summer long Raffi played in the shade of Father Oak's green leaves with his friends, Chip and Blackbird.

On the first day of autumn Raffi woke early,
ready to play. He left a morning kiss on his
mother's whiskers, and tiptoed out to find Chip.

But where were Father Oak's leaves?
All Raffi could see was a silvery mist.

When he crept to the end of the branch,
he saw that the leaves were still there — but wait!
There was a pretty golden leaf amongst the green.
Should he pick it? Would Father Oak mind?

Suddenly the leaf dropped, twirling away in the mist.

"Maybe Father Oak wants me to have it!"
As Raffi scampered after it another leaf
dropped out of the mist, then another:
one, two, three, four – more and more!
Raffi rushed to catch the leaves,
but there were too many.

Was something wrong with Father Oak?
The chilly mist made Raffi shiver.
"Maybe Father Oak is cold too!" he thought.
So he gathered the leaves, and piled them into
a blanket over Father Oak's roots.
Just then Chip peeked round Father Oak's trunk.

"Raffi, what are you doing?" asked Chip.
"I'm making a blanket for Father Oak. He's losing
his leaves because he's cold," answered Raffi.
"It's a lovely blanket," said Chip, "but look —
the leaves are still falling. Maybe he's crying."
"Father Oak must be sad. Let's hug him better!" said Raffi.

The friends put their arms around Father Oak
and hugged him. But still the leaves fell.
"Blackbird, come and help us!" called Raffi.
"Father Oak is crying, so let's hug our hugest hug
and sing our happiest song!"

Their singing woke Raffi's mother.

"What's happening?" she asked.

"Father Oak's crying all his leaves away and
we're trying to cheer him up!" they cried.

"Don't worry, little ones. He isn't crying," she said.

"He's telling us that autumn is here and
winter is coming," Raffi's mother explained.
"What is winter?" they asked.
"Winter is a cold, dark, sleepy time when all
the leaves and flowers hide away," she said.
"Winter sounds horrible!" said Raffi.
"But without winter there would be no room
for spring," said his mother.
"Everything would be tired and always the same."

"What shall we do with Father Oak's
leaves then?" asked Raffi.
"We'll make our own blankets for our
Winter Sleep," said his mother.
Soon all the animals were busy gathering
leaves and food for their winter stores.

Through golden autumn days they ate and ate,
until they were fat as could be.
"Is it time for our Winter Sleep yet?" Raffi asked.

"Not quite," said his mother. "We still have one
more job to do." And she gave Raffi five acorns.

"We must make beds for them," she said.
So they dug five little holes and tucked
them snugly in the ground.
"What will happen?" asked Raffi.
"They'll sleep all winter, just like us," she said,
"and when spring comes . . . wait and see!"

Then they curled up together in their
den, and Raffi's mother sang a winter
lullaby until Raffi fell sound asleep.

Snug inside Father Oak they
drowsed away dark days of wind . . .

and ice . . .

and snow.

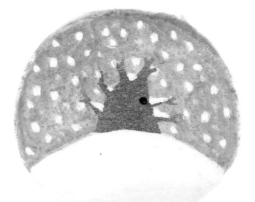

One morning, Raffi woke to a tingle in the air.
He poked his nose out of the den . . .
Father Oak's branches sparkled with tiny new leaves.
"Mummy!" he shouted. "I think it's spring now!"
She rubbed the sleepy-dust from her eyes
and peeked out.

"Are our acorns awake yet?" she asked.
They peered down and there, on the
ground below, was a wonderful surprise:
from each little bed they had dug,
two tiny oak leaves pushed up into the sun.
"Look!" cried Raffi excitedly.
"Our acorns have turned into baby oak trees!"

"So they have," smiled his mother.
"And if you help Father Oak look after
them, one day they will become
big oak trees – just like him!"